GREAT MOMENTS IN OLYMPIC HISTORY

Olympic Ice Skating

C. Farbs

New York

To Monty: for schlepping the kids to the rink—and all those other places . . .

Published in 2007 by The Rosen Publishing Group, Inc.
29 East 21st Street, New York, NY 10010

First Edition

Library of Congress Cataloging-in-Publication Data

Farbs, C.
Olympic ice skating / C. Farbs.
p. cm. — (Great moments in olympic history)
Includes index.
ISBN-13: 9781-4042-0969-5
ISBN-10: 1-4042-0969-7 (library binding)
1. Skating—History—Juvenile literature. 2. Winter Olympics—Juvenile literature. 3. Figure skaters—Juvenile literature. 4. Women figure skaters—Juvenile literature. I. Title.
GV850.223.I34 2007
796.91—dc22

2006024236

Manufactured in the United States of America

On the cover: East German figure skater Katarina Witt performs at the 1988 Calgary Olympics. She later won the gold medal.

CONTENTS

CHAPTER 1

The Origins of Ice Skating

Ice skating has been around for thousands of years. The oldest pair of ice skates found is more than 5,000 years old. It is believed that skating originated in the northern European countries of Norway, Sweden, Finland, and the Netherlands. In these areas with long winters, ice skating was once the fastest mode of transportation across frozen rivers and lakes. About 1,200 years ago, Viking hunters and warriors commonly made skates out of reindeer antlers or ox and elk bones. They drilled holes into each end of the antler or bone. Leather straps were looped through the holes and attached to sandals. In fact, an old Dutch word for skate is *schenkel*, which means "leg bone." Since it was difficult to stand on early skates, skaters used poles for balance and to push themselves forward.

In the thirteenth century, the Dutch communication and transportation systems often relied on skaters who went from village to village along frozen waterways. It was the Dutch who first began using wooden skates with long iron blades in the thirteenth or fourteenth century. Sharp and sturdy iron blades allowed skaters to move more quickly and without poles. Eventually, skating spread across Europe and became a favorite winter pastime and sport.

Made of wood, iron, leather, and fiber, these ice skates were used in the United States during the mid-1800s.

Speed Skating

One of the earliest forms of competitive skating was speed skating. In this sport, skaters compete to determine who is the fastest over a certain distance. Speed skating is also the sport in which competitors move the fastest on a flat surface without mechanical aid. This speed makes the sport exciting to watch. Speed-skating competitions were held in the Netherlands as early as 1676.

By the eighteenth century, speed skating had become a popular sport across northern Europe, with numerous competitions held throughout the winter months. In 1763, what may have been the world's first organized speed-skating race was held in England. It covered a distance of about 15 miles (24 km). About a century later, in 1876, the first man-made ice rink—called the Glaciarium—was built in London.

In 1889, the first speed-skating World Championships for men were held in the Netherlands. It was also in the Netherlands that the International Skating Union (ISU) was created in 1892. To this day, the ISU is the official organization governing all competitive skating. It makes rules and trains and certifies judges. It also decides how international competitions, including the Olympics, are to be run.

Skating Comes to North America

In the early nineteenth century, European immigrants brought their skates with them when they crossed the Atlantic Ocean. By the mid-nineteenth century, skating had spread across North America. E. W. Bushnell of Philadelphia, Pennsylvania, was the first to make a lighter, sharper, and longer all-steel blade in 1850. Bushnell's invention revolutionized skating, since light, strong steel blades did not have to be sharpened as often as iron blades. They allowed skaters to make complicated moves and sudden turns on the ice. Meanwhile, one of the earliest recorded ice skating races in North America took place on Canada's St. Lawrence River in 1854. Three British army officers raced each other 168 miles (270 km) along the frozen river from Montreal to Quebec City.

Long-Track Speed Skating

Olympic speed skating, or long-track speed skating as it is known today, made its debut at the first Winter Olympics in 1924 in Chamonix, France. It has been a highlight of the games ever since. Two skaters compete by sprinting around a 400-meter oval track with two lanes for distances of 500, 1,000, 1,500, 5,000, or 10,000 meters. The winner is the skater with the fastest time, measured to the hundredth of a second. Scandinavians dominated the 1924 and 1928 Olympic competitions, although Americans and Canadians were challenging rivals. Originally, only men competed in speed skating. Although women participated in speed skating as a demonstration sport from the 1932 Olympics onward, women's speed skating didn't become a competitive event until the

Canada's Clara Hughes (in red and black) and Claudia Pechstein of Germany race in the 5,000-meter women's speed skating final at the 2006 Olympic Games. Hughes captured the gold medal.

1960 Winter Games in Squaw Valley, California. That year, Soviet skater Lidiya Skoblikova proved how fast a woman could skate.

Today's Olympic champions often reach speeds of 35 miles (56 km) per hour. They move in a crouched position that allows them to make long, powerful strides and complete quick crossovers in corners. In recent years, American skaters such as Eric Heiden, Bonnie Blair, and Dan Jansen have captured fans' hearts and won numerous gold medals while setting impressive world records.

Short-Track Speed Skating

Short-track (or indoor) speed skating originated in North America in the early twentieth century. Unlike long-track speed skating, in which two competitors at a time race against the clock, short-track speed skating involves four to eight skaters sprinting around a 111-meter rink, each attempting to be the fastest of the group. Although not as favored as long-track speed skating in Europe, short-track speed skating is extremely popular in both the United States and Canada.

At the 2006 Turin games, South Korea took home the gold medal in the men's 5,000-meter short-track relay, beating the Canadian team.

While many international competitions existed, this form of speed skating first became an Olympic event at the 1992 Winter Games in Albertville, France. Americans and Canadians have long excelled at the sport. More recently, however, skaters from Japan, South Korea, and China—whose Yang Yang (A) brought China its first ever Winter Games gold—have been challenging

A Collision Course

Skaters' lightning speed, coupled with the possibility of collisions, make short-track speed skating particularly exciting to watch. Short-track is known as the "demolition derby" of the Olympics. Instead of competing for the best time, skaters compete against each other. They race full speed around a tight oval track, bumping each other as they battle to reach the finish line first. Wipeouts are frequent and sometimes brutal. Because of the danger involved, the sides of the track are cushioned to soften collisions.

Short-track skaters wear special protective gear. Goggles shield their eyes from ice chips, and hard plastic helmets and knee, shin, and neck guards protect against other injuries. Thick gloves are especially important because hands are placed on the ice for balance when rounding curves, and nobody wants their fingers run over by a rival's sharp blade.

their dominance. [The "A" is used to distinguish Yang Yang from another Chinese skater with the same name, who is known as Yang Yang (S).]

Figure Skating

One of the most eagerly anticipated events at each Winter Games is figure skating. This immensely popular sport first emerged in Europe in the early 1770s. Traditional "figure skating" involved tracing a series of geometric shapes that were based on the figure 8. The "father of figure skating" as we know it was an American skater and ballet teacher named Jackson Haines. In the 1860s, Haines changed the sport by adding music and incorporating ballet and other dance movements.

Haines's style of skating was not well received in America. He moved to Europe, where it became immensely popular. In spite of this, competitive figure skating didn't take off until the late 1800s. Organized by the ISU, the first men's World Championship was held in 1896 in St. Petersburg, Russia. The first World Championship for women took place in 1906 in

This portrait of Jackson Haines, the "father of figure skating," dates back to 1912.

Davos, Switzerland. In 1908, pairs skating was introduced at the World Championship. The first Olympic figure-skating competitions took place at the 1908 London games. Figure skating was performed on an indoor rink, which allowed the event to be featured in the Summer Olympics. When separate Winter Olympics began to be held in 1924, figure skating became a part of the Winter Games.

Among the earliest Olympic figure-skating champions were two Scandinavians. Gillis Grafström was a Swedish skater who captured more Olympic medals than any other figure skater. He later coached multiple medal-winner Sonja Henie of Norway. In the 1950s, Canadian and American stars exploded onto the scene with athleticism and innovative techniques. Americans Dick Button and Tenley Albright left their mark on the sport. In the 1960s, America's "ice princess" Peggy Fleming turned figure skating into one of the most watched sporting events on television. In the 1980s, figure skating's popularity grew even more due to the star-making performances of Canadian Brian Orser, East German Katarina Witt, and Americans Brian Boitano and Debi Thomas.

Pairs Figure Skating

In the 1950s, after 40 years of not competing in the Olympics, the Soviet Union began sending athletes to compete in the games. Soviet pairs figure skaters offered an unbeatable combination of elegance and athleticism. One of the greatest skaters in pairs skating was Irina Rodnina. In 1972, 1976, and 1980, Rodnina won gold medals, first with Aleksey Ulanov and then with Aleksandr Zaytsev. In fact, through 2006, a Soviet or Russian duo has won the gold medal at every Winter Olympics since 1964. This is the longest winning streak in modern sports history.

Aleksandr Zaytsev lifts Irina Rodnina as they perform their gold medal–winning routine at the 1977 European Figure Skating Championships in Helsinki, Finland.

Ice Dancing

Unlike pairs figure skating, ice dancing resembles ballroom dancing and requires couples to move in time to the rhythms of selected music. It also limits the lifts partners may perform and does not allow the throws and jumps that characterize pairs skating. The first ice dancing world championship was held in 1952. The greatest early ice dancers were often British. However, at the 1976 Olympics—where ice dancing was first introduced as a competitive event—Soviet couples won all three medals. In fact, Soviet skaters won every ice dancing medal until 1984. That year, the unforgettably perfect performance of British pair Jayne Torvill and Christopher Dean won the gold medal. A unique blend of art and sport, ice dancing is a captivating Winter Olympic event.

From a practical method of transportation to an awe-inspiring form of athleticism, skating has proven to be a lasting pastime. As future Olympic skating stars improve upon modern techniques, they call to mind the past skating stars who helped mold skating into one of today's most exciting sports.

Jayne Torvill and Christopher Dean captured the bronze medal at the 1994 Olympics in Lillehammer, 10 years after winning the gold medal.

CHAPTER 2

The Early Stars of Figure Skating

Figure skating is the oldest Winter Olympic sport. Its first appearance was at the 1908 Summer Games in London, where the competition was held on an indoor rink. It is also one of the most glamorous sports, although it wasn't always that way. Early figure-skating competitions focused on skaters' abilities to skate "compulsory figures." This means that each skater was required to trace certain geometric shapes. One of the most basic of these was the figure 8. Skating geometric figures demanded precision and control, but it was not very creative for athletes or thrilling for spectators.

The Great Innovator

Figure skating became more exciting with the arrival of Swede Gillis Grafström. Grafström invented some of the sport's most famous movements, such as the spiral, the flying sit spin, and the grafström spin. He was also the first skater to perform the famous and difficult axel jump in competition. His inventiveness and willingness to take risks didn't go unrewarded. To this day, Grafström remains the figure skater with the most Olympic medals.

Grafström first competed in the 1920 Summer Olympic Games in Antwerp, Belgium. Despite breaking a skate at the last minute, which forced him to borrow an old-fashioned model with "curly toes," he received top marks from all six judges and won the gold medal. Grafström repeated his gold-medal performance at the 1924 games in Chamonix, France, and the 1928 games in St. Moritz, Switzerland, where he won despite skating with a swollen knee. During the 1932 games at Lake Placid, New York, Grafström seemed ready to win yet another gold. However, during the compulsory figures, he became confused over which figure to trace. This kept him from capturing a fourth gold medal. Nonetheless, Grafström won the silver medal.

Figure Skating's First International Star

Gillis Gräfstrom's contributions to figure skating didn't end in 1932. He later trained one of Olympic figure skating's legends: Sonja Henie. Norway's Henie was only 11 years old when she made her Olympic debut at the Chamonix games in 1924. Nervous and insecure, she kept interrupting her free-skating performance to ask her coach for advice. As a result, the small blonde skater finished last.

Henie would never come in last again. From then on, her family spared no expense in her training, which included private rinks, expert skating coaches, and ballet lessons. When she returned to the games in 1928, 15-year-old Henie won the gold medal and revolutionized the way female skaters presented themselves. Traditionally, female skaters wore long skirts and black skates. Henie skated in short skirts that gave her the freedom to do complicated jumps and spins. Her fur-trimmed costumes and white skates brought a sense of glamour to the sport.

Henie wasn't all looks—she was action, too. Before she competed, figure skating had been a sport in which skaters moved while music played in the background. Henie changed that with elegantly choreographed programs in which her sits, spins, and leaps followed the rhythms of a carefully selected piece of music. Her talented routines led her to repeat her gold-medal win at the 1932 Lake Placid games and again at the 1936 games in Garmisch-Partenkirchen, Germany. By this time, she was 23 and so popular that police were needed to control crowds when she appeared publicly throughout Europe and North America.

Taking Chances for the Gold

World War II (1939–1945) interrupted the Olympics. After the 1936 games, no more games were held until the 1948 Olympics in St. Moritz, Switzerland. By then, American and Canadian figure skaters had begun to challenge Scandinavian domination of the sport. One of the brightest of these new talents was an

Hollywood's Skating Star

After the 1936 Olympic Games, the world's first international figure skating star—Sonja Henie—went to Hollywood, California. She became one of the most popular movie stars of the late 1930s and early 1940s. In more than a dozen films, she delighted audiences with her charming accent and graceful moves on ice. Henie is shown below with actor Tyrone Power in the movie *Second Fiddle*. Offscreen, she created and starred in the Sonja Henie Hollywood Ice Revue, a figure-skating exhibition that toured across North America and turned the skater into a multimillionaire. Her longtime coach, Frank Carroll, said Henie "made skating something that every little girl wanted to do."

American named Richard Button. Dick Button was only 18 in 1948 when he became the first American male to win an Olympic gold medal in figure skating. He did this by being the first person to complete a double axel jump in competitive skating. At the time, the move—one of the most famous jumps in figure skating—was very new. Button had only succeeded in doing it for the first time 2 days before competition. On the day of the event, he decided to take a chance. Button said of the historic perfect jump, "The lift was strong, the revolution certain and the landing sure."

Dick Button was in his first year at Harvard University when he struck Olympic gold for the first time at the 1948 games.

Button's daring performance wasn't a one-time occurrence. Four years later at the 1952 Winter Games in Oslo, Norway, he again decided to take a chance. Although he had the lead, Button didn't want an easy victory. He was determined to do a difficult jump known as the triple loop. No skater had ever performed any kind of triple jump in competition. Once again, the risk paid off. Button performed the new move with such skill and ease that all the judges declared him winner of the gold medal.

A Surgeon's Story

Another young, brave American talent who captured the gold as well as the hearts of Olympic fans everywhere was Tenley Albright. A surgeon's daughter, Albright received her first pair of ice skates when she was 8. Unfortunately, at the age of 11, she developed polio, a sometimes crippling disease. It was thought she might never walk again. During her recovery, doctors recommended that she build up her strength by doing something she loved. Tenley Albright began figure skating again.

Albright skated so well that she won a silver medal at the 1952 Oslo games. She returned to the 1956 Olympic Games in Cortina, Italy. Less than 2 weeks before the Olympics, she hit a bump in the ice during her training. As she fell, her left skate cut into her right ankle. The sharp blade tore through three layers of her boot, slashed a vein, and badly scraped the bone. In fear and pain, Albright sent for her surgeon father. He arrived 2 days later and patched her up. Despite her injury, Albright skated well enough to earn first-place votes from ten out of eleven judges and win the Olympic gold medal. Following her triumph, Tenley Albright returned to the United States, enrolled in Harvard Medical School, and went on to become a famous surgeon—just like her father.

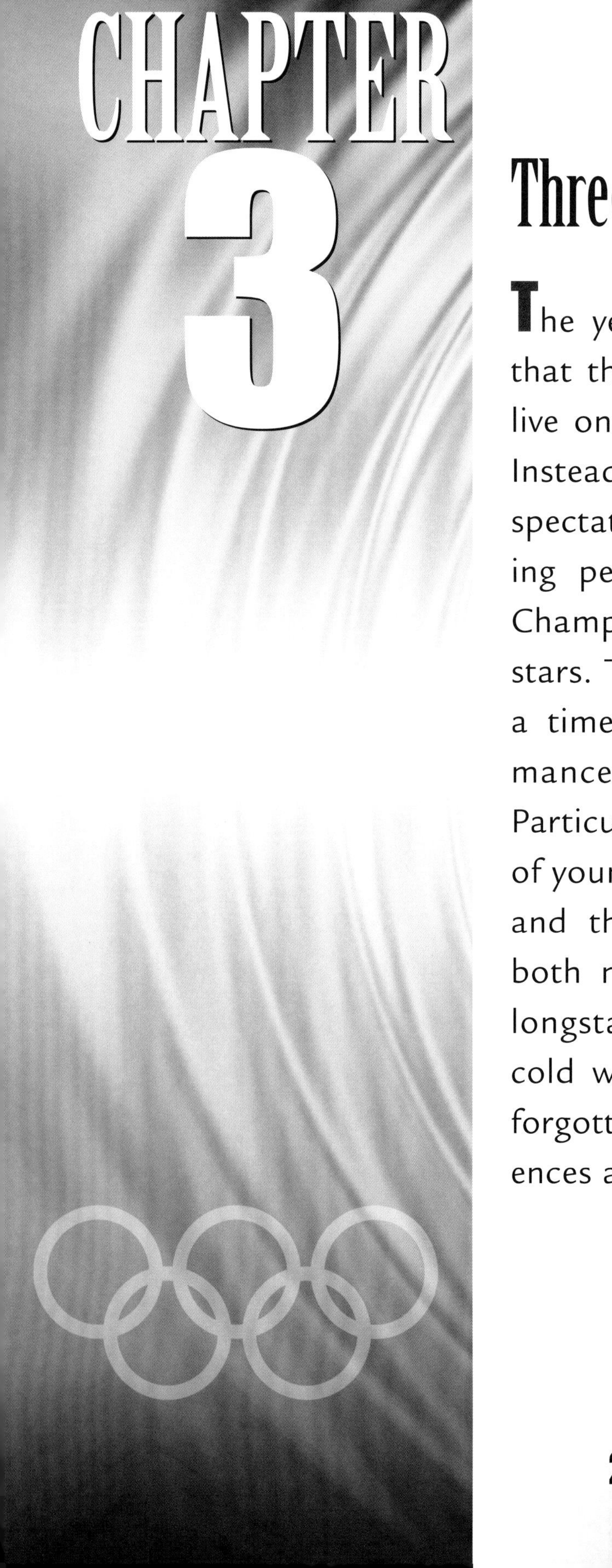

Three Unforgettable Women

The year 1960 marked the first time that the Winter Olympics were shown live on television in the United States. Instead of hundreds, now millions of spectators could watch athletes' amazing performances as they happened. Champions now became recognizable stars. The 1960s and early 1970s were a time of memorable skating performances by unforgettable women. Particularly remarkable were a handful of young skaters from the Soviet Union and the United States. At the time, both nations were in the midst of a longstanding conflict known as the cold war. However, the cold war was forgotten as the performers awed audiences and fellow competitors alike.

Woman of Speed

Women's speed skating was first introduced at the 1932 Olympic Games as a demonstration sport. It wasn't until the 1960 games in Squaw Valley, California, that women were allowed to compete for medals. Ready to take advantage of speed skating's newly competitive status was 20-year-old Soviet skater Lidiya Skoblikova.

For most athletes, capturing two gold medals in one Olympic Games would be the triumph of a lifetime. However, when Skoblikova won the gold medal in both the 1,500-meter and 3,000-meter speed skating events at Squaw Valley, she was only warming up. Four years later, she returned to the games in

In February 1964, Soviet speed skating champion Lidiya Skoblikova won the 3,000-meter long-track speed skating competition, the sixth gold medal of her Olympic career.

Innsbruck, Austria. She was favored to win the long-distance 1,000-meter, 1,500-meter, and 3,000-meter races, but not the 500-meter sprint. Over 4 days, Skoblikova amazed spectators, setting an Olympic record by a large margin in the 1,500-meter and taking the gold medal in all four women's speed skating events! She was the first person to win four gold medals in a single Winter Games. Skoblikova is also the only woman to win a total of six Olympic gold medals in individual events. Her triumphs made Soviet citizens and women all over the world proud.

America's Skating Sweetheart

Lidiya Skoblikova's impact on women's speed skating in the 1960s was matched by the overwhelming popularity of young American figure skater Peggy Fleming. Despite having little money, Peggy Fleming's family was determined to fulfill her dream of becoming a great figure skater. Her father relocated the family twice so his daughter could have better training. Fleming's mother designed and sewed all her skating costumes. Training and determination paid off when Fleming qualified for the 1964 games in Innsbruck, Austria. She placed sixth. However, it was her 4-minute free-skating performance at the 1968 Olympics in Grenoble, France, that earned her a gold medal and won her fame.

Fleming's free-skate program combined artistic expression with powerful athleticism. Her performance was shown live and in

Looking Back

For Americans, Peggy Fleming's 1968 victory was particularly sweet. The nation was still mourning a 1961 airplane crash that killed the entire U.S. figure skating team, including Peggy's coach and all of her role models. Fleming's gold medal was the first U.S. gold figure skating medal since 1960 and America's only gold medal at Grenoble. Figure skating was as popular as professional football that year. Linda Leaver—future gold medalist Brian Boitano's figure skating coach—said, "Her energy got the train of U.S. figure skating moving again. Once it got rolling, nothing has stopped it since." At the time, Fleming had no idea of her importance. She later admitted, "I wish I had been aware of the impact my career would have. I think I might have taken it all a lot more seriously."

color to television viewers around the world—an Olympic first. The world was enchanted with this beautiful 19-year-old skater who had sacrificed so much and worked so hard to make her dream come true.

Change of Partners

Lidiya Skoblikova was one of the first Olympians to reveal the talent of Soviet skaters to the world. However, from the 1960s onward, the event in which Soviet skaters truly excelled was figure skating. Among the many legendary figures, perhaps none stands out more than Irina Rodnina. To this day, she is considered one of the top figure skaters and one of the best pairs skaters in history. Rodnina's Olympic fame was the result of being part of not just one legendary pair, but two!

Soviet pairs figure skater Irina Rodnina is pictured at center wearing her gold medal, in front of her first partner, Aleksey Ulanov, in 1972.

Irina Rodnina began her career skating with fellow Soviet Aleksey Ulanov. The first time they entered the World Championships in 1969, they won the gold medal. They also succeeded in defeating the Protopopovs, the reigning Soviet Olympic champions. While the Protopopovs were graceful and elegant, Rodnina and Ulanov were inventive and daring. For the next 3 years, they won every major pairs figure skating tournament, including the Olympic gold medal at the 1972 games in Sapporo, Japan. Shortly after, Rodnina and Ulanov broke up their partnership when Ulanov decided to skate with another member of the Soviet team.

Rodnina's sudden single status left both her and the Soviet Union in despair. Following her split from Ulanov in 1972, a nationwide hunt for a new partner began. The result of this search was a tall, athletic Soviet skater named Aleksandr Zaytsev. With Zaytsev, Rodnina proved that she could be a champion with any skilled partner. Together they revolutionized pairs skating, turning their backs on the more sentimental, romantic programs that had dominated the event in favor of more technically innovative, fast-paced routines. They later married and went on to win every competition they entered, including Olympic gold medals at the 1976 Innsbruck games and the 1980 Lake Placid games.

CHAPTER 4

Surprises and Upsets

Part of the draw of competitive skating is that it is such a suspenseful sport. If skating is so fascinating to watch, it is because winning a competition depends on many factors. To win a gold medal, skaters have to be not only strong, athletic, and fast, but also precise and graceful. Concentration and timing are just as important as physical power. The difference between winning and losing can also depend upon the sharpness of steel blades, the surface of the ice, and just plain luck. The history of the Olympics is filled with stories of disappointment, determination, surprising upsets, and unexpected defeats.

Fast Times

The first time that long-track speed skater Eric Heiden competed in the Olympics was in Innsbruck, Austria, in 1976. Only 17 years old, he finished seventh in the 1,500-meter race and nineteenth in the 5,000-meter race. Disappointed but determined, he spent the years before the 1980 games winning the World Championships 3 years in a row. He then arrived in Lake Placid, New York, and won gold medals in all five speed skating events, from the 500-meter to the 10,000-meter. He set an Olympic record in every event!

Particularly dramatic were the 500-meter and 1,500-meter races. In the first race, the world-record holder, Soviet skater Yevgeny Kulikov, was in the lead until he slipped slightly, allowing Heiden to sprint ahead in the last crossover to a surprise victory. In the 1,500-meter race, Heiden was in the lead until he hit a rut in the ice halfway through the race and almost fell. Without missing a beat, Heiden quickly recovered and went on to beat another world-record holder, Norway's Kai Arne Stenshjemmet, by 0.37 second!

The night before the 10,000-meter competition, Heiden attended the U.S.–Soviet Union hockey game. When the U.S. team won, he was so excited that he had trouble falling asleep and ended up missing his wake-up call. Leaping out of bed in a panic, he hurriedly grabbed a few pieces of bread and dashed to the rink. This last-minute rush didn't stop Heiden from winning his final

Fame Never Went to Heiden's Head

At the 1980 Lake Placid games, Eric Heiden won more gold medals than the combined athletes from twelve countries, including Finland, Norway, Switzerland, Canada, and Japan. Although American fans went wild, the muscular midwesterner was unimpressed by his victories and sudden fame. "Heck, gold medals, what can you do with them?" he said after winning his fifth race. "I'd rather get a nice warm-up suit. That's something I can use. Gold medals just sit there."

race or from breaking the world record by an impressive 6.2 seconds. Heiden accomplished what no Olympian had ever done before—he won five individual gold medals in a single Olympics!

Dynamic Dancing Duo

Soviet couples had been dominating Olympic ice dancing since it was introduced in 1976. Then British couple Jayne Torvill and Christopher Dean arrived at the 1984 Sarajevo Olympics in Yugoslavia. (Sarajevo is in that part of the former Yugoslavia now known as Bosnia and Herzegovina.) They redefined ice dancing with a flawless, dramatic performance that was theatrical and athletic. Torvill and Dean skated to Maurice Ravel's *Boléro*, a passionate musical piece about two people in love who throw themselves into a lava-filled crater because they can't be together. By the time the music ended and the couple lay still on the ice, the rink seemed transformed into a volcano as applause thundered from the audience. Then everything fell quiet as they waited for the scores. The couple earned perfect artistic scores from the judges and won the gold medal. Their performance was so emotional that afterwards a reporter asked the couple if they planned to marry. "Well, not this week," replied Dean.

Torvill and Dean's use of *Boléro* almost didn't happen. While Ravel's original composition is over 17 minutes long, Olympic rules declared that the free-dance performance had to be 4 minutes long (plus or minus 10 seconds). Determined to use the piece, Torvill and Dean asked a music arranger to cut it down to a shorter version. The best the arranger could do was to reduce the piece to 4 minutes 28 seconds. Frustrated by the extra 18 seconds, the British couple reread the Olympic rulebook and discovered that the timing of a routine began only when the skaters started skating. Their solution? To begin their performance sitting on the ice, locked in an embrace, while moving their bodies to the music. After 18 seconds had gone by, they began to skate—and to make skating history.

To train full-time for the 1984 Sarajevo games, Christopher Dean gave up his job as a police officer while Jayne Torvill quit her job selling insurance.

"Battle of the Brians"

One of the greatest "battles" in Olympic skating history was between two figure skaters named Brian at the 1988 Calgary games. Going into the Olympics, Canada's Brian Orser was favored to win. The world champion that year, he represented his country's best chance for a gold medal at the first Winter Olympics held in Canada. Expectations were high months before the games. Orser was hounded by reporters and fans alike. Even at his local supermarket, people would stop to cheer for him. The pressure to win was so great that Orser said he felt ready to pop.

Brian Boitano of San Francisco, California, was a talented skater who had been a rival of Orser's for several years. In Calgary, Boitano and Orser had very close scores after the first part of the figure-skating event. For the second part—the free skate worth 50 percent of the final score—Boitano skated first. He performed perfectly except for one flaw: a slight wobble in a triple-jump landing. The stage was set for Orser to win his expected gold medal. However, 90 seconds into his routine, Orser almost missed a triple flip jump, which caused him to land on two feet instead of one. Shaken, he was forced to follow with a double axel jump instead of the more spectacular triple axel he had planned. Although their scores were very close, Brian Boitano ended up winning the gold medal, returning to the United States an Olympic hero.

Brian Orser (left) and Viktor Petrenko of the Ukraine (right) stand with gold medalist Brian Boitano at the 1988 Calgary Olympics.

Looking Back

Years after the "Battle of the Brians," the two former rivals are friends who often skate together in ice shows and on television. In fact, they admit that their Olympic face-off brought them closer.

Brian Boitano explained in an interview, "After all, we shared an experience that no one else could understand and we'll be linked forever because of it." Besides, Boitano couldn't forget the past even if he wanted to. At a hotel in Hamilton, Canada, in 2005, the American skater was approached by a man who said, "You're the Brian who beat our Brian!"

Getting over it was more difficult for Brian Orser, who couldn't imagine life without a gold medal for a long time. For years, he wondered to himself, "What if?" Then, one day he saw a tape of the event and realized his performance had been quite good. "We both skated really well. The drama unfolded according to script," confessed Orser. "Of course, I would have written a different ending."

"Witt"-ing Performances

Considered one of the greatest figure skaters of all time, Katarina Witt dominated women's figure skating throughout the 1980s. Just as memorable as her artistic performances were Witt's beauty and grace. At the time, female athletes from Communist countries—like Witt's East Germany—seemed so serious. As performers, they tended to emphasize their athleticism more than their elegance. With her glittery costumes, Witt was a breath of fresh air. Of course, it helped that she was very talented. At the age of 18, having never won a world championship, Witt arrived at the 1984 games in Sarajevo and found herself skating against two world champions. Although American Rosalynn Sumners was favored to win, Witt surprised her rival by landing three triple jumps in the free skate. She beat Sumners by 0.1 point to capture the gold medal.

No other figure skater had won back-to-back gold medals since Sonja Henie, but Witt hoped to do so at the 1988 Calgary games. She and popular American skater Debi Thomas led after the compulsory figures and short program. The intense

East German Katarina Witt gave a dramatic gold medal performance at the 1988 Calgary Olympics.

competition between the two young women was increased by the fact that both had chosen music from the opera *Carmen* for their free skate. Witt skated well enough to win her second gold medal, leaving Thomas with the bronze medal and Canadian Elizabeth Manley with the silver medal. Thomas's bronze medal made her the first African American athlete in the history of the Winter Olympics to win a medal.

Following her Calgary triumph, Katarina Witt became the first East German skater to turn professional. However, when the Olympic rules changed to allow professional skaters to compete alongside amateurs, she returned once again to skate in the 1994 Olympics in Lillehammer, Norway. Aware that this time she would not win any medals, Witt concentrated on a performance whose artistry would be unforgettable. At the time, Sarajevo, where she had won her first Olympic gold medal 10 years earlier, had been devastated by war. As a message of peace, Witt's performance to the folk song "Where Have All the Flowers Gone?" was one of the most moving routines in Olympic figure skating history.

In 1988, American Debi Thomas became the first African American to win a medal at the Winter Olympics.

Overcoming the Odds

Sometimes the most unforgettable Olympic moments have less to do with winning medals than displaying the courage, determination, and ability to overcome almost impossible odds. Whether faced with financial hardship or bad luck, a referee's unfair call or a sudden accident, skaters who still manage to excel offer some of the finest examples of Olympic spirit. They also provide some of the most memorable stories in Olympic history, showing that being a champion is about more than just winning a medal. How many of us would have the courage and determination of Bonnie Blair, Dan Jansen, Yang Yang (A), or Zhang Dan?

A "Queen" and Her Jewels

From the very beginning, it seemed as if Bonnie Blair was destined to become the "Queen of Speed Skating." While her mother was giving birth to her in the hospital, her father had taken his five older children—four of whom were amateur skaters—to a skating competition. When Bonnie was only a few hours old, the competition was interrupted for an announcement over the loudspeaker: "It looks like [the Blair] family has just added another skater."

The prediction quickly came true. By the age of 4, Bonnie was already participating in speed-skating competitions. While her skating siblings abandoned the sport, Bonnie was determined to go all the way to the Olympics. As a teenager, she wanted to qualify for the 1984 games but believed her chances depended on training in Europe. When lack of funds threatened to dash her hopes, a police charity in Blair's hometown of Champaign, Illinois, raised the entire amount needed. Though she attended the 1984 Sarajevo Olympics, it wasn't until the 1988 Olympics in Calgary that she earned the title "Queen of Speed Skating."

At the Calgary games, Blair's first event was the 500-meter race. From the sidelines, she watched world-record holder Christa Rothenburger of East Germany break the 500-meter speed skating record. Impressed but confident, she went out on the ice and improved on Rothenburger's time by 0.02 second with her long strides. She not only won her first gold medal, she set a new world record of 39.10 seconds. Bonnie's winning streak had begun. At the 1992 games in Albertville, France, she won gold medals in both the 500-meter and 1,000-meter speed skating events. Then she

The Blair Bunch

In Calgary, there were about thirty of them cheering from the stands. In Albertville, about forty-five of them, dressed in purple team jackets, sang "My Bonnie Lies over the Ocean." And in Lillehammer, more than sixty of them traveled across the ocean to see Bonnie make Olympic history. Known affectionately as the "Blair Bunch," these faithful friends and family members of America's fastest female speed skater formed one of the Olympics' most memorable cheerleading squads. Says Bonnie, "A lot of people think that I'm under a lot of pressure with my family and friends spending all that money to follow me. But they don't care whether I win or lose. They'd come anyway because we're one big family that's having lots of fun." Speed skater Dan Jansen is pictured here with some members of the Blair Bunch.

returned to the 1994 Olympics in Lillehammer and once again captured gold medals in both events, winning each race by a large margin. Of all the prizes Blair won, perhaps the one that meant the most to her was the necklace made for her by a jeweler in Champaign. It was set with thirty-nine jewels—one for each of the 39 seconds of Blair's first world record.

Beating Bad Luck

In 1984, 18-year-old American long-track speed skater Dan Jansen attended his first Winter Olympics. Finishing fourth in the 500-meter, he missed winning a bronze medal by 0.17 second. For a young man just starting out, Jansen had done well. Determined to do even better in the next Olympics, Jansen trained hard and was expected to win at the 1988 Calgary games. Then, on the morning of the day he was to race in the 500-meter event, his sister, Jane, died from leukemia. Despite his grief, Jansen prepared himself to win the race for Jane. It seemed as if he would triumph until he fell 100 meters into the race. Four days later, in the 1,000-meter event, he was closing in on a gold medal and a world record when he fell again.

Never one to give up, Jansen returned to the Olympics in 1992. Once again, however, he failed to win any medals. He finished fourth in the 500-meter race and twenty-sixth in the 1,000-meter race. Disappointment overwhelmed him. Yet, he still wasn't ready to

American skater Dan Jansen was crushed when he crashed out of the men's 500-meter speed skating race at the 1994 Olympics in Lillehammer.

hang up his skates. He kept his sights on winning a gold medal. He had won many world championships and set a number of world records. When the 1994 Lillehammer games rolled around, Jansen, now 28, knew that this would be his final chance. Still considered a favorite in the 500-meter, Jansen was skating well when he again slipped on the ice. He didn't fall, but he was out of the running for a medal.

Jansen wouldn't let another setback stop his drive to win. Four days later, he faced the last Olympic race of his life and his very last chance at a medal. Unfortunately, he was competing in the 1,000-meter race, which had never been his strongest event. Calling upon all his strength and courage, Jansen shot from the starting line and more than halfway through the race was on his way to setting a world record. Suddenly, he stumbled, causing spectators to gasp in horror. This time he recovered rapidly. He not only finally captured his first gold medal after

With his daughter Jane in his arms, Dan Jansen celebrates his record-breaking victory in the 1,000-meter speed skating race at the 1994 games.

10 years of trying, but also set a world record! When he skated his victory lap with his baby daughter, Jane (named for his sister), his fellow Olympians and the 10,000 fans in the stands went wild with applause.

Gold for China

In the mid-1990s, Asian skaters began to leave their marks on a sport that had been dominated by Americans, Canadians, Dutch, Scandinavians, and Russians. Short-track speed skating, which became a competitive event in the Winter Olympics in 1992, had become particularly popular in China, Japan, and South Korea. One of the brightest new talents to emerge from these nations was a Chinese speed skater named Yang Yang (A).

Yang was a world champion in the 500-meter and 1,000-meter events and was favored to win both when she entered the 1998 Olympics in Nagano, Japan. She was off to a promising start in the 500-meter quarterfinals, but her hopes were dashed when she was disqualified for cutting off another skater. Yang called it the worst moment in her skating career. Things didn't go much better in the 1,000-meter race. At first, Yang set a world record in the quarterfinals and then defeated Korea's defending Olympic champion, Chun Lee-Kyung, in the semifinals. In the finals, Yang was surging ahead for most of the race. At the last turn, Chun slipped and thrust her leg across the finish line to capture the gold. Yang was disqualified from winning the silver medal after she was accused of blocking Chun with her arm. As the games came to a close, Yang was frustrated. Yet she remained convinced that better times would come.

When Yang returned to the 2002 Olympics in Salt Lake City, Utah, her first event was the 1,500-meter race. Unfortunately, she

Chinese short-track speed skater Yang Yang (A) surges ahead to win the 1,000-meter race at the 2002 Olympics.

missed winning a medal by less than 0.1 second. This setback, however, would be the last she would experience. Fueled by determination, Yang skated to victory in the 500-meter and captured her first gold medal. After winning a silver medal in the relay, she skated in the 1,000-meter event, where she won another gold medal. Yang's wins marked the first time a Chinese athlete had ever struck gold at the Winter Olympics.

Unforgettable Silver

Perhaps the most memorable moment at the 2006 Olympics in Turin, Italy, came not from the Russian couple who won the gold medal for pairs figure skating, but from the Chinese couple who captured the silver medal. When Zhang Dan and her partner, Zhang Hao, took to the rink, their Russian rivals, Tatiana Totmianina and Maxim Marinin, had just completed a program that put them in line for the gold medal.

Zhang and Zhang's only shot at victory was to take a great risk and attempt a jump so difficult that it had never been performed in competition: a throw quadruple salchow. However, when the moment came, instead of completing

Chinese figure skating pair Zhang Dan and Zhang Hao are shown here performing a throw at the 2006 games. Moments later, Zhang Dan crashed to the ice.

Zhang Dan is helped to her feet by Zhang Hao. Despite a severely injured knee, she was determined to continue the competition.

four revolutions in the air, Zhang Dan fell to the ice headfirst and went smashing into the boards. As her partner, Zhang Hao, dashed to her side, thousands of stunned and fearful spectators held their breath.

The pair's chances of an Olympic medal seemed to be crushed. However, after a few minutes spent talking to a doctor and then skating around the ice, they surprised the crowd and fellow Olympians by picking up their program where they had left off. In spite of Zhang Dan's intense pain, the brave couple completed their program, including all the remaining jumps and throws. Although they couldn't surpass the Russians, their silver medal, accompanied by a standing ovation, rewarded Olympic courage at its best.

Showing courage and true Olympic spirit, Zhang Dan and Zhang Hao raise their arms in victory after capturing the silver medal.

Skaters, Past and Present

Ice skating has certainly come a long way since ancient Scandinavian hunters and warriors first strapped animal bones to their boots and skated across frozen lakes and rivers. Today's skates consist of lightweight boots that mold to skaters' feet for a perfect fit. Attached to these are blades of the highest quality steel that have been cut to razor-thin sharpness using lasers. Scientists are still at work designing better, faster skates. Who knows what records will be broken or how performances will change in future Olympic games?

Technology aside, competitive skating has become a physical sport requiring great power and precision, as well as an art that showcases skaters' elegance and creativity. Perhaps skating is so exciting to watch—particularly at the Olympic level—because of the drama involved. The ever-present possibility of slipping, hitting a bump, or wiping out creates a permanent state of suspense. Will the skaters soar or crash? To the spectators who watch, breathless, as these talented athletes compete, the real pleasure is in witnessing the magic of a human gliding over frozen water.

Timeline

1908 Figure skating, the oldest of the Winter Olympic sports, makes its debut at the Summer Olympic Games in London, England.

1920 Antwerp, Belgium. Sweden's Gillis Grafström wins his first Olympic gold medal for figure skating.

1924 Chamonix, France. Gillis Grafström wins his second gold medal. Long-track speed skating for men makes its Olympic debut.

1928 St. Moritz, Switzerland. Gillis Grafström wins his third gold medal. Norway's Sonja Henie, 15, wins her first gold medal.

1932 Lake Placid, New York. Gillis Grafström wins a silver medal. Sonja Henie wins her second gold medal.

1936 Garmisch-Partenkirchen, Germany. Now an international skating star, Sonja Henie wins her third gold medal and goes to Hollywood.

1948 St. Moritz, Switzerland. Richard "Dick" Button completes a double axel jump and becomes the first American male to win an Olympic gold medal in figure skating.

1952 Oslo, Norway. Dick Button wins his second gold medal. American figure skater Tenley Albright wins a silver medal.

1956 Cortina, Italy. Tenley Albright captures the gold medal in figure skating.

1960 Squaw Valley, California. Women's speed skating is a competitive event for the first time. Soviet speed skater Lidiya Skoblikova captures two gold medals.

1964 Innsbruck, Austria. Lidiya Skoblikova becomes the first person to win four gold medals in a single Winter Olympics.

1968 Grenoble, France. Peggy Fleming captures a gold medal and makes figure skating one of the most popular sports in America.

1972 Sapporo, Japan. Soviets Irina Rodnina and Aleksey Ulanov capture the gold medal in pairs figure skating.

1976 Innsbruck, Austria. Ice dancing makes its Olympic debut. With her new partner, Aleksandr Zaytsev, Irina Rodnina captures a second gold medal in pairs figure skating.

1980 Lake Placid, New York. Irina Rodnina and Aleksandr Zaytsev win another gold medal in pairs figure skating. Eric Heiden takes home gold medals in all five speed skating events, setting an Olympic record in each one.

1984 Sarajevo, Yugoslavia. Britain's Jayne Torvill and Christopher Dean win a gold medal in ice dancing. East Germany's Katarina Witt captures her first gold medal.

1988 Calgary, Canada. The "Battle of the Brians" results in Brian Boitano taking home the gold. The United States' Debi Thomas becomes the first African American athlete to win a medal at the Winter Olympics. In speed skating, America's Bonnie Blair captures her first gold medal.

1992 Albertville, France. Bonnie Blair wins gold medals in the 500-meter and 1,000-meter events. Short-track speed skating makes its Olympic debut.

1994 Lillehammer, Norway. Bonnie Blair captures gold in the 500-meter and 1,000-meter speed skating events. American speed skater Dan Jansen captures a gold medal in the 1,000-meter event.

1998 Nagano, Japan. China's short-track speed skater, Yang Yang (A), is disqualified from the 500-meter and 1,000-meter events.

2002 Salt Lake City, Utah. Yang Yang (A) wins two gold medals and a silver medal in short-track events.

2006 Turin, Italy. Chinese figure skater Zhang Dan flies out of her partner Zhang Hao's arms and crashes against the boards. The couple manages to win a silver medal.

Glossary

axel jump A figure-skating jump in which the skater takes off from the forward outside edge of one skate, spins, and lands on the back outside edge of the opposite skate. A single axel is $1\frac{1}{2}$ revolutions, a double is $2\frac{1}{2}$, and a triple is $3\frac{1}{2}$. Named for its inventor, Axel Paulsen.

choreographed Referring to the planned movements that performers make to music.

Communist Referring to a system of government in which the government owns all means of production.

compulsory Required.

crippling Describing an illness that can cause permanent damage to the body, especially the legs.

crossover An area halfway through each lap in which speed skaters change lanes.

free skate Also sometimes called the long program, the free skate does not have required elements. Skaters select their own music and jumps, spins, and footwork to best display their technical and artistic skills. The free skate is $4\frac{1}{2}$ minutes long for men and pairs, and 4 minutes long for women and ice dancers.

innovative Inventive, original.

leukemia A cancer of the blood and bone marrow that causes a buildup of blood cells that do not function properly.

lift A pairs figure-skating move in which the man fully extends one or both arms to hold up his partner.

loop A figure-skating jump in which a skater takes off from the back outside edge of one foot, spins, and lands on the same back outside edge.

ovation A recognition of a good performance by applause.

polio A disease in which the nerve cells of the lower part of the brain and spinal cord become inflamed. Some people who get the disease hardly seem ill at all. Others become very sick and may become paralyzed.

salchow A jump named after its Swedish inventor, early twentieth-century skating champion Ulrich Salchow. A skater jumps off the back inside edge of one skate, spins, and lands on the back outside edge of the other skate.

short program The first part of a figure-skating program with eight compulsory elements that must be performed to music by all competitors in no more than 2 minutes and 40 seconds.

Soviet Union Short name for the Union of Soviet Socialist Republics (USSR), which included Russia and fourteen surrounding nations. From 1922 to 1991, all were under the control of one central Communist government.

spin A figure-skating move in which skaters rotate, or spin, while one or both skates remain on the ice.

spiral A figure-skating move in which a skater glides along the ice on one skate and extends their nonskating leg behind them into the air.

throw A pairs figure-skating move in which the woman is thrown into the air, completes one or more revolutions, and lands skating backwards.

For More Information

Ice Skating Institute
17120 N. Dallas Parkway
Suite 140
Dallas, TX 75248-1187
(972) 735-8800
http://www.skateisi.com

International Skating Union
Chemin de Primerose 2
CH 1007
Lausanne, Switzerland
(41) 21 612 66 66
http://ww2.isu.org

Skate Canada National Office
865 Shefford Road
Ottawa, Ontario
K1J 1H9
Canada
(888) 747-2372
(613) 747-1007
http://www.skatecanada.ca

U.S. Figure Skating Headquarters
20 First Street
Colorado Springs, CO 80906
(719) 635-5200
http://www.usfsa.org

United States Olympic Education Center
Northern Michigan University
1401 Presque Isle Avenue
Marquette, MI 49855
(906) 227-2888
http://usoec.nmu.edu

World Olympians Association
Regional Office of the Americas
The Biltmore
1200 Anastasia Avenue, Suite 140
Miami, FL 33134
(305) 446-6440
http://www.woaolympians.com

Web Sites

Due to the changing nature of Internet links, the Rosen Publishing Group, Inc., has developed an online list of Web sites related to the subject of this book. This site is updated regularly. Please use this link to access the list:
http://www.rosenlinks.com/gmoh/ices

For Further Reading

Cohen, Sasha, with Amanda Maciel. *Sasha Cohen: Fire on Ice: Autobiography of a Champion Figure Skater*. New York: HarperCollins Children's Books, 2006.

Hill, Anne E. *Michelle Kwan*. Minneapolis, MN: LernerSports, 2004.

Macy, Sue. *Freeze Frame: A Photographic History of the Winter Olympics*. Washington, DC: National Geographic Society, 2006.

Morrissey, Peter. *Ice Skating*. New York: Dorling Kindersley Publishing, 2000.

Ohno, Apolo Anton, with Nancy Ann Richardson. *A Journey: The Autobiography of Apolo Anton Ohno*. New York: Simon and Schuster Books For Young Readers, 2002.

Wukovits, John. *The Encyclopedia of the Winter Olympics*. New York: Franklin Watts, 2001.

U.S. Olympic Committee. *A Basic Guide to Figure Skating*. Irvine, CA: Griffin Publishing Group, 2001.

U.S. Olympic Committee. *A Basic Guide to Speed Skating*. Irvine, CA: Griffin Publishing Group, 2001.

Bibliography

Skating: Olympic Sport Since 1908
http://www.olympic.org/uk/sports/programme/index_uk.asp?SportCode=SK
Skate History.ca
http://www.skatehistory.ca
Skate Today
http://www.skatetoday.com
The Virtual Ice Skates Museum
http://www.iceskatesmuseum.com
U.S. Speedskating
http://www.usspeedskating.org
Top N. American Athletes of the Century
http://espn.go.com/sportscentury/athletes.html
Ice Skating
http://www.encyclopedia.com/doc/1E1-iceskati.html
About Speedskating
http://www.speedskating.ca/eng/about
Torino 2006: Olympics History
http://www.cbc.ca/olympics/history

Index

About the Author

C. Farbs hails from Saskatoon, Saskatchewan. Like many Canadians, she grew up looking forward to the winter months, during which she could ski, skate, and toboggan down icy slopes. After completing her undergraduate degree in psychology and education at Vancouver's University of British Columbia, she went to work in the public school system, specializing in remedial reading. Still an avid skier and skater, C. Farbs currently lives on Vancouver Island.

Photo Credits

Cover, pp. 8, 41 © Robert Laberge/Getty Images; p. 5 (top) © Collection of New York Historical Society, USA; p. 5 (bottom) © Kari Marttila/Alamy; p. 7 © Al Bello/Getty Images; p. 9 © Gerry Penny/AFP/Getty Images; p. 10 © George Grantham Bain Collection, Prints and Photographs Division, Library of Congress; pp. 12, 23, 24 © Staff/AFP/Getty Images; pp. 13, 38 © Shaun Botterill/Allsport; p. 17 © Pictorial Parade/Getty Images; pp. 18, 21 © Allsport/Hulton Archive; p. 28 © AFP/AFP/Getty Images; p. 29 © Phil Cole/Allsport; p. 31 © Daniel Janin/AFP/Getty Images; p. 32 © Mark Cardwell/AFP/Getty Images; p. 33 © Jerome Delay/AFP/Getty Images; p. 36 © Brian Bahr/AFP/Getty Images; p. 39 © Clive Brunskill/Getty Images; p. 40 © John MacDougall/AFP/Getty Images; p. 42 (top and bottom) © Franck Fife/AFP/Getty Images.

Designer: Daniel Hosek
Editor: Therese Shea